DORA the EXPLORER

I Love My Papi!

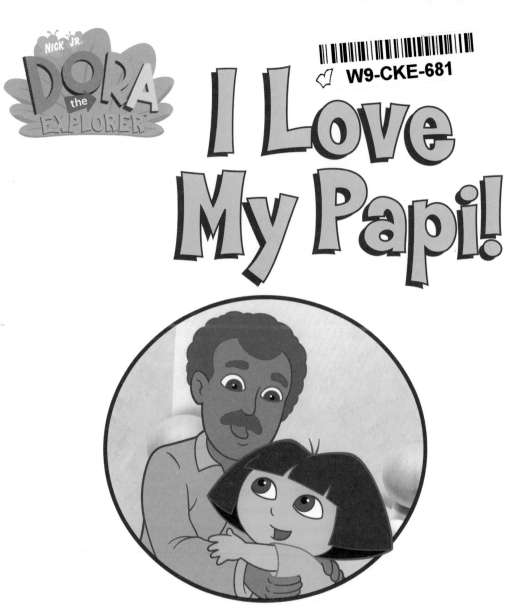

by Alison Inches
illustrated by Dave Aikins

SCHOLASTIC INC.
New York Toronto London Auckland Sydney
Mexico City New Delhi Hong Kong Buenos Aires

My  **PAPI** and I love to do things together!

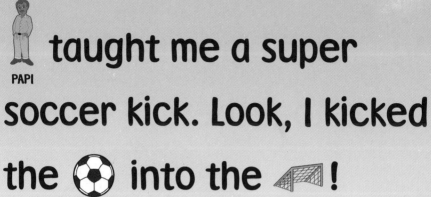 taught me a super soccer kick. Look, I kicked the  into the !

PAPI

SOCCER BALL

GOAL

We also love playing  .

BASEBALL

PAPI coaches my team.

He taught us how to
swing the  and slide

BAT

into home ⬠.

BASE

On weekends  and I
ride together.

PAPI

BIKES

Or sail on a .

BOAT

Sometimes we go to the 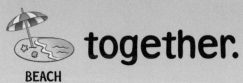 together.

BEACH

We build giant and
SAND CASTLES

play in the .
WAVES

My  is a really good .
PAPI   COOK

He taught me how to bake

a special  and make
          CAKE

yummy .
       SANDWICHES

Sometimes we pack a  PICNIC

and share it with my

friend 🐵.
BOOTS

My made us this swing! He can build anything with 🧰.

PAPI

TIRE

TOOLS

One time  took us to
the 🎪.

PAPI

🐵 loved the 🤡.

CIRCUS   BOOTS   CLOWNS

Then bought us and

PAPI **POPCORN**

  for a treat.

STRAWBERRY **ICE CREAM**

Yum! Yum!

At the end of every day  **PAPI** tucks me into BED .

Then we read a .
BOOK
I like 📚 about 🐮🐷.
BOOKS   ANIMALS

says, "I love my !"
PAPI **DORA**

And I say, "I love my !"
PAPI